# THE RETURN OF THE CHRISTMAS WITCH

**DAN MURPHY & AUBREY PLAZA**

*illustrated by* **JULIA IREDALE**

VIKING

VIKING

An imprint of Penguin Random House LLC, New York

First published in the United States of America by Viking,
an imprint of Penguin Random House LLC, 2022

Visit us online at penguinrandomhouse.com.

Library of Congress Cataloging-in-Publication Data is available.

Manufactured in Italy

ISBN 9780593350836

10   9   8   7   6   5   4   3   2   1

LEG

Book design by Jim Hoover and Julia Iredale
Typeset in Fairy Tale, Decour Black, Sequel, and Australis Pro
The illustrations in this book were created with gouache and digital mediums.

*For my grammy, Mary, for her storytelling, and my sister, Stephie, for her bravery.*   —D. M.

*For Natalie and Renee, my sister witches for life.*   —A. P.

*For Grandad.*   —J. I.

## The Christmas Witch was dreaming.

For hundreds of years, buried deep in the ice, she had slept while the world changed around her, dreams swirling through her head like snowflakes. In them, she saw those she had known—Lutzelfrau, Elsmere, Malachi. The animals of the wood, the people in the small towns she'd visited.

Her brother . . .

Just now, Lutzelfrau was leading her through the forest to a grove of trees, where bright, blazing flowers grew beneath them. The woods were as peaceful as she'd remembered, until suddenly all of the trees were on fire, burning red and orange.

"Arise, Kristtörn, arise!" Lutzelfrau was whispering to her. She looked up and saw Malachi circling overhead as the sun grew brighter . . .

The vision faded away. She awoke, staring up at the sky as little flakes hit her eyes. The ice that had once surrounded her had melted into a pool of slush. She looked around to where her home had stood. Nothing remained now but a mound of snow.

"How long have I been asleep?" she wondered, as she pushed herself up and looked at her reflection in the ice. She was startled to see that years of slumber had stripped the red color from her hair, for it was now white as the snow; her once emerald eyes were a dull jade.

In her palm she was grasping a sprig of holly that had withered and turned brown. She concentrated for a moment to revive it, but she could not summon that old familiar tingling in her fingers. In fact, she could feel no magic coursing through her veins at all. It was then that she came to the sad realization: not only was she alone, but she had lost all of her powers.

A wind picked up, and the snow became heavier. She began walking many miles through the growing blizzard, until she saw in the distance what appeared to be a mighty gray fortress. On its side, a single word was illuminated in red like a beacon: KRINGLE.

*Kringle!*

*My brother must live here,* Kristtörn thought as she ran in the snow toward the building.

She pushed open the metal door and stepped into a cavernous room. It was filled from floor to ceiling with tidy red-and-green packages. More traveled on a conveyer belt along the room's edge, each one stamped with the word KRINGLE. Kristtörn marveled at this modern technology, the likes of which she'd never seen before. It at last dawned on her that she must have been frozen for centuries.

Furious thoughts raced around inside Kristtörn's head. She couldn't believe that her brother had abandoned Christmas. Had the holiday become so focused on presents that he had forgotten her and their mutual purpose? Her disappointment slowly turned into a familiar rage. Just then, the ship blew its horn, and Noah ran to the window.

"I've got to get these last packages on that ship before it takes off." Noah sighed. "Sometimes I miss the simple Christmases from when I was a boy, don't you, Miss . . . ?"

But when he turned around, Kristtörn was gone, and so was the sack of presents.

**A little while later,** the ship blasted its horn again and pulled out to sea. The Christmas Witch was on board, hidden away in some netting. She looked back to the shore.

There in the snow, a mountain of packages had been set ablaze. They had been arranged to spell out words that could be read all the way from the ship:

**The Christmas Witch** was fast asleep on the deck as the ship snaked its way up the Atlantic. She dreamt she was a child again, laying in her bed in the little house with the thatched roof, looking up at the same stars she now sailed under. She was ill, and Lutzelfrau was tending to her. From the hole in her floor, she watched the old woman empty a sack of mushrooms into her large pot on the fire. As she stirred, she spoke these words:

> *Turkey tail and lion's mane, and now the charm is wound!*
> *Reishi, lingzhi, heal the pain, the ties are tightly bound!*

She continued chanting as a cloud of smoke filled the entire house, and then she was there beside Kristtörn in the haze. "But, Mother, how do I get my powers back?" Kristtörn asked.

"Shhh, shhh, you must rest now, my child," Lutzelfrau answered. "That will come in time. Here, eat this!" And she offered her spoonful after spoonful of hot mushroom soup . . .

**When she awoke,** the ship had docked in a port on the Delaware Bay. Down below, men and women unloaded box after box from the ship's hold. Kristtörn threw a rope ladder over the railing and dropped quietly into the water, swam to the bank of the river, and disappeared among the trees.

The night was dark, starless, and silent as she stumbled through the woods. The bare trees formed an eerie canopy overhead. No birds nestled in their branches. No squirrels or foxes or even mice stirred in the dry leaves at her feet. The forest hardly seemed alive.

At last, a solitary nighthawk landed on the path in front of her. "Excuse me, where am I?" she began, but the nighthawk just screeched and flew off. She pressed on.

It wasn't long before she saw a faint light in the distance, and by and by she came upon a large old house with light glowing from within. She drew closer and peered curiously through a window. Inside, a family was having dinner, and it seemed that some kind of commotion was afoot.

**Poppy Piper,** a precocious young girl, was causing a scene at the dinner table. It had all started when Grammy Piper, visiting for the evening, began reminiscing about Christmases past . . .

"When I was little, Santa Claus was as real as you and me," she confided to Poppy's twin brother, Peter, who had made a tray of Santa-shaped sugar cookies for dessert. "Every year, my mother would take me to the department store at Christmastime to see old Santa for myself."

"And you really, really saw him?" asked Peter breathlessly.

"Indeed I did!" Grammy answered. "And you know something? Every Christmas he brought me exactly what I asked for. Back in those days, it wasn't the number of gifts that mattered; it was that Santa brought you something special."

Bernadette, Poppy and Peter's mother, rolled her eyes at her husband.

"Wow!" said Peter in amazement. "How did he know what you wanted?"

"Well, that was his magic," Grammy recalled, as Peter stared wide-eyed at his Santa cookie. "Somehow, he was always listening. Of course, we had our own ways of sending him messages, too. In fact, I used to have a—"

"Now, Grammy, you're making that up," Mrs. Piper interrupted. "You never saw or talked to Santa Claus."

"Think he'll ever come back, Grammy?" Peter asked.

Poppy finally exploded. "Oh, don't be so silly, Peter. If there ever was a Santa Claus, he's long gone now."

"Poppy, sit down," her mother said. "Don't yell at your brother."

"Yeah, Poppy. If you're bad, you won't get anything for Christmas!" Peter teased.

"I don't care," Poppy replied angrily. "Santa was a fraud. He didn't care about anyone. He sold out to Dad's awful company and ruined Christmas forever!"

Peter's eyes welled up with tears. He looked sadly at the cookie in his hand.

"Poppy, go to your room!" Mrs. Piper said sternly. "And stay there until I tell you to come out." Poppy pushed back her chair from the table and ran up to her room, slamming the door.

**Long after the rest** of her family was asleep, Poppy lay awake in bed, thinking back on the day. Maybe there had been a Santa, a long time ago. And maybe, deep down inside, she wished he would come back, too. She felt bad for yelling at Peter.

Outside the wind howled through the trees. And suddenly Poppy heard a *scratch scratch scratch*ing at the window. She tiptoed across the floor. But when she threw open the curtains, there was no one there.

Below in the yard, in the light of the waning moon, Poppy thought she saw the pale face of a woman staring up at her from behind a large oak tree. Frankie, the family collie, began barking down in the kitchen, and Poppy turned away from the window, just for a second. When she turned back, the face was gone.

**That night, in** the woods nearby, the Christmas Witch found herself in a world she no longer recognized. She made a meager meal out of a few old beets and carrots she had pulled from a vegetable garden, then settled into a bed of leaves nestled between two fallen sycamores. She cupped her hands to whistle the song of the nightingale but even that was too tiring. *I must find the Kringle headquarters,* she thought to herself, *and hopefully my brother will be there.* But before she finished her plan, she was fast asleep.

**Kristtörn awoke to** the sounds of a brass band coming from the nearby road. A large crowd had formed to watch a parade passing by.

As Kristtörn made her way toward the crowd, a young woman dressed as an elf handed her a flyer. It read: COME SEE KRIS KRINGLE AT THE WINTER FESTIVAL! Kristtörn stared back at the jolly face and the twinkling eyes in the picture. This must be a sign!

The parade disappeared out of sight and the crowd dispersed, and the Christmas Witch continued into town. It was a cold little town,

the buildings sleek, modern, and lifeless, adorned only with icy silver lights and large posters of Santa that whipped about in the breeze. Nowhere was there any greenery to be found, no boughs crossing the streets or wreaths on the lampposts. The people she passed, all with vacant eyes and dull expressions, walked by her as if she were a ghost. She hurried down side streets, following the arrows pointing to the Winter Festival's entrance, until finally the sounds of festive holiday music reached her ears.

The fair was alive with activity and all around Christmas was for sale. In one pavilion, an elf with a long beard was enticing fairgoers to view the latest model of an automated sleigh used to deliver presents across the world—the Kringle SleighMaster 900. Its curved, teardrop shape was punctuated by a red light that both acted as a guiding beacon and contained a laser to scan the barcodes on the chimneys of houses.

"Step right up! *Admire* its sleek design! *Wonder* at its speed. *Marvel* at its ability to enter your home—without you ever knowing!"

Kristtörn moved on, observing the rows and rows of Kringle gift-ordering kiosks that conveniently led toward the exit, and shook her head at what Christmas had become. There was no sign of Kris Kringle himself. Her brother really had abandoned Christmas, and in her heart, she knew he was far away from here. Then she noticed, in the distance, a tent she felt strongly drawn to, labeled ANIMAL MENAGERIE.

Once inside, she made her way along the tent wall until she came to a big brass cage with a sign:

Kristtörn peered through the bars of the cage, where sat a reindeer, large and majestic, with gray fur about his face and a sad look in his eyes. The beast moved toward her, and she stuck her hand through so he could lick it. He looked deep into her eyes with a slight glimmer of recognition, but alas she couldn't communicate with him. *If only I could ask him about Santa*, she thought as she petted his silvery mane. But then she recoiled in shock by what she saw next to the cage.

On the other side of Donner was a large, shiny block of ice stand-ing on a wooden pedestal, with a plaque that read: A PRESERVED CREATURE FROM THE ANCIENT WORLD. In the center of the block, a black macaroni penguin with colorful feathers and a sweet face, frozen in time . . .

*Elsmere!* Her trusty friend had also been captured in ice. When she realized he was now on display for all to see, she began to cry. She wept until she heard voices moving toward the tent. Quickly, she ran out and disappeared into the crowd.

**The sun was** already low in the west, casting an orange glow into the frosty sky, when Poppy made her way home from school. As she walked along, she played an old Christmas tune on her achipiquon, a flute that her Lenape grandfather had carved and given to her. She passed through her front gate, around the house and right to an old shed at the back of the property. This was where she kept her prized collection of old ham radios—ancient gadgets that her grandfather had taught her to love. After he died, her grammy had passed them on to her. She spent her time tinkering with the parts and sliding the dials in hopes of catching a signal. Someday, she dreamed, she would have a real radio show of her own. But for now, she loved to come out here where no one would bother her (especially Peter) and pretend to broadcast to the world.

"Good afternoon, listeners, whoever and wherever you are. You're listening to Poppy on the Radio."

"As many of you know, the Kringle Winter Festival is in town this week, and among their many other assaults on the Christmas holiday, they claim to have one of Santa's own reindeer on display. In a cage," she added with emphasis. "That poor creature should be roaming free at the North Pole with his other brothers and sisters, but instead he's locked up!"

"And as Kringle continues to forget the true spirit of Christmas, I want to make a special request today: Santa Claus, if you really are out there somewhere, please fly here and save this holiday from what it has become. Poppy Piper, over and out!" Even though pretending to broadcast made her feel a little silly, it also made her feel less alone.

Flute in hand, Poppy started back toward her house but stopped when she noticed a mysterious plume of smoke rising from the marshes beyond the woods.

The leaves crackled under her feet as she hurried through the wintery twilight. When she drew closer she was surprised to see a woman in the middle of the marsh grass. She was peculiar looking, wrapped in a dirty blanket with a shock of long white hair, and most certainly not from around here. She appeared to be brewing something in a large kettle over a fire.

Poppy watched this strange woman. Where did she come from? And what in the world was she doing back there? Then all of a sudden, she heard Frankie's barks echoing through the woods, and the spell was broken.

"Poppy? Pop-py!" Her mother always sang her name like a melody. *Maybe if I ignore her, she'll go away*, thought Poppy.

"PENELOPE ROSE PIPER! You come on home now!" shouted her mother. She knew that tone well. Reluctantly Poppy turned and ran back toward her house, deciding not to tell her mother about the woman in the marsh.

**Lutzelfrau was still** coming to Kristtörn in her dreams, but the old witch had not yet revealed how she could reclaim her powers. She hoped brewing some dandelion tea might do the trick. "Mother, if you can hear me, send me a sign!" Kristtörn implored, poking the dandelion petals. But no sign came.

She noticed growing beside the log she was sitting on a cluster of mushrooms, small and white and knobbly. She had hated the taste of them since childhood, but she was so ravenously hungry that she plucked one and ate half of it. Immediately, she felt a twitch in her fingers like invisible lightning, but she was too hungry to notice. After a few more bites, she tossed the rest in the bay. Reenergized, she knew what she must do next.

**Night fell.** The Winter Festival closed down and the workers went to bed. All was quiet and still. From the shadows of the fairground, the Christmas Witch crept silently until she reached the tent of the Animal Menagerie.

She slipped inside and made her way along the wall until she came at last to Elsmere.

"My poor, loyal friend," she whispered. "I will get you out of here, I promise you."

"Madam, did you say something?" came a gruff voice from behind her. She turned quickly, but there was no one in the room except the old reindeer, rising unsteadily to his feet. He shook the dust from his great antlers, one of which she noticed now was broken.

"You . . . heard me?" Kristtörn replied, equally surprised.

"Yes! Only one other human has ever been able to speak with me, and that was Santa Claus himself . . ."

"I am Kristtörn," she said. "Santa's sister."

"Oh my! In that case, I am Donner," he said with a little bow. "I do remember you. Once, long ago, we came to visit you at the South Pole. I served your brother for many years, until I joined this miserable festival."

"How horrible, to be locked up like this. And where is my brother? I must find him!"

The old deer shook his head and replied, "I do not know. But please, and if you are indeed who you say, might you free me? I have been trapped here for far too long."

"Yes, of course!" answered the witch, taking a large set of keys off of a hook on the wall nearby and unlocking the door of the cage. The reindeer walked out and nuzzled her hand in appreciation.

"Look what they've done to my poor friend Elsmere," she said, gesturing toward the block of ice. Just then, there was a rustling in the far corner of the tent.

"Quickly, hop on my back," the reindeer cried. "We must get out of here!" The witch climbed on, and she and Donner galloped out of the tent and into the moonlight.

From the shadows, Poppy, carrying a flashlight and a crowbar, stared after them, amazed by what she had just seen.

Once they reached the woods, Donner slowed down and Kristtörn hopped off of his back to walk along beside him. He offered everything he knew about the new world.

"As you can see, evergreen trees and bushes don't grow around here anymore, not for a long, long time."

"So that means no Christmas trees? How sad!" Kristtörn exclaimed.

Donner sighed. "The humans have done away with all of those customs. Several years ago, one of Santa's head elves took over the entire delivery of Christmas gifts. Santa must have agreed to this because before we knew it, Christmas was forever changed. He disappeared shortly thereafter."

"But why? What would have possessed my brother to do that?"

"All I know is that I was awoken early one morning and sent by truck to the Kringle Headquarters. And now every November, the other animals and I spend the winter months traveling with the fair from town to town."

"This is so typical of my brother. Only thinking of himself, and always leaving people behind! He has been doing it since we were born," she fumed.

"As I said, I don't know how much Santa had to do with—"

"The blame lies with him! You, who served him well for many long years, you should have been protected. He had a responsibility to you, and he has a responsibility to Christmas!"

"That is true," said the reindeer thoughtfully. "If you please, Madam Witch, I am very hungry. They only feed us stale oats at the festival. Could we stop for food?"

"Of course."

"Wild mushrooms would suit me just fine, and I can smell them nearby!"

And before long they reached the edge of the marshland. There among the tall grasses, they discovered a fairy ring of mushrooms, shimmering in the moonlight. When Old Donner had eaten his fill of mushrooms, they both lay down for a rest. She buried her head in the soft folds of the deer's back and fell asleep.

**Meanwhile, the Christmas Witch** grew increasingly frustrated. Despite being able to talk to Donner, she remained otherwise powerless. One evening, lost in thought and nibbling on some gingerbread cookies that the little girl had left for her, Kristtörn stared at Donner devouring mushrooms from the forest floor. For the first time she noticed that as he ate each one, another grew immediately in its place. And she suddenly remembered the rest of the words Lutzelfrau chanted in her dreams:

*Turkey tail and lion's mane, the charm is tightly wound!*
*Reishi, lingzhi, heal the pain, the ties securely bound!*
*Through the earth the roots endure, within thy hands the power restored,*
*Connect them through the ground!*

Eagerly, she stuck her hands deep into the soil in the middle of the fairy ring. A power surged through her, from the tips of her fingers to the ends of the strands of her hair. She laughed for the first time in centuries, electrified by the enchanted earth.

The power knocked her backward into the grass. Emboldened, she touched the soil, concentrating with all her might, until a small green bud sprouted at the place where her finger met the ground. A new holly bush was beginning to grow.

"Are you okay, Madam?" Donner asked with his mouth full.

"I am more than okay—the Christmas Witch has finally returned!"

She was anxious to further test her powers, so she summoned Donner to her side. She wrapped both of her hands around his broken antler and focused. It took a few minutes, but then she felt the power racing forth from her hands, and his antler grew until it was as big and as strong as ever.

"Aha, you see!" she exclaimed, leaping over rocks and bushes excitedly while Donner admired his antlers in the reflection of the water. "And now to the task at hand!" She would find her brother—and there would be no stopping her this time—even if it meant destroying Christmas altogether.

"What task would that be?" Donner asked nervously, noticing the strange look in her eyes.

The Christmas Witch threw back her head and pointed toward the moon.

"The only way to get my brother's attention is to send him a powerful message in the sky where he cannot ignore it!" She filled her cauldron with salty bay water, and spoke these words as she stirred:

*Mist of darkness, fill the air,*
*Hand of nightshade, lock of hair.*
*Shroud the land, as black as night,*
*Some witch hazel to blind the sight.*
*Pinch of wolfsbane, ounce of coal,*
*Bunch of hemlock in the bowl.*
*To the brew, now add these three:*
*Mistletoe, holly, and bay berry!*

The cauldron bubbled and a thick black mist rose up from the water. The cloud grew and the Christmas Witch blew on it, spreading it through the woods.

Day after day, the dark cloud continued to grow and settle in the streets. Schools and shops were forced to close, people stayed home, and cars took to the streets at their own peril. There was an eerie quiet as the ghostly mist blanketed the town.

**Finally, it was** the day before Christmas. The fog had grown
so dark and thick and unrelenting that the SleighMasters could no
longer operate. Instead, the Kringle employees were forced to work
overtime driving trucks around town, hand delivering packages. But
even this proved nearly impossible in the black mist. On the news,
there was talk of postponing Christmas until a warm front came
through, or canceling it this year altogether.

Poppy spent Christmas Eve feeling anxious. She was out in her shed
again, tinkering with her grammy's magic red telephone, making one
last plea for Santa to return. For who else could navigate such fog? But
all she got was static.

There was a knock on her door. "Poppy, open up!" It was Peter. "You have to come inside. Dad hasn't come home yet, and Mom is worried."

Poppy was worried about her father, too. He was out there in the fog, trying to deliver the last batch of Christmas presents for Kringle. Deep down, she feared that this might be the work of the Christmas Witch.

"In a minute, Peter. This is my last message to Santa before tonight."

"Oh, Poppy, Santa isn't real. You said so yourself," Peter scoffed. "It's silly to spend every day out here talking to imaginary people on these old machines. They don't even work! No one is listening!"

Angry tears stung Poppy's eyes. "Leave me alone, Peter!" she said, and she shoved him out the door.

Dinner came and went, and still there was no sign of Mr. Piper. Afterward, Poppy grabbed her coat and slipped out the back door.

She made her way through the fog, so dense she could barely see the lantern in front of her, but she soon came to the edge of the marsh. There, the Christmas Witch sat in front of her cauldron, still blowing on the smoke. When the witch saw Poppy she raised her eyebrows in surprise.

"What are you doing here, little girl? You shouldn't be out in this fog alone."

"Please, Ms. Witch," Poppy said bravely. "If you are behind this, please make this stop. It has gotten out of hand. You're going to ruin Christmas!"

The Christmas Witch threw back her head and laughed.

"But of course I am!" she shrieked. "Santa has abandoned Christmas, and now he must pay for it!" Poppy couldn't understand it. She thought the witch loved Christmas as much as she did. She had even left Poppy a sprig of real holly that very morning.

"Besides, you're too late! The fog is unstoppable now. It's been spreading across the country, and it will soon destroy this wretched holiday once and for all."

"But . . . but my father is out there in that fog. What if he can't find his way home?"

The Christmas Witch's face softened for a moment. "I'm sorry, child. But this must be done. I have spent years searching, only to be betrayed again and again. No, it ends here and now. Santa Claus alone must fix this!"

Poppy turned to run away, but suddenly—

A distant jingling floated through the air. Poppy and the Christmas Witch looked up into the sky. Through the clouds, a red glow appeared, circling overhead.

"It . . . it can't be . . ."

But it was. "Donner!" the Christmas Witch called. "Come, we must fly." Donner galloped up obediently. He could not deny the witch anything now. She hopped on his back. "I am going to face my brother and see this to the end!"

"Please—stop!" Poppy cried.

"On, Donner!" she commanded. He made a running leap, and together they took off into the sky, quickly disappearing into the fog.

**Donner and the Christmas Witch** soared through the clouds toward the red glow, which grew brighter and brighter until finally the shape of a sleigh and a team of reindeer appeared. As they approached, the Witch whistled through the haze.

For a moment—silence. But then the familiar melody was returned, echoing through the clouds. It was a welcome sound, beautiful and yet sad. Kristtörn used her powers to clear the mist ahead by creating a funnel of wind and snow around her, Donner, and the rapidly approaching sleigh. There, suspended in the sky, she came face-to-face with her brother.

"Kristtörn!" Her name floated through the air. Her brother had greatly aged since she had last seen him, yet his cheeks remained rosy and his eyes bright. "My darling sister, I thought you were lost forever!"

The witch only scowled. She had no time for pleasantries. "Why did you abandon Christmas, brother? And why have you forgotten *me*?"

Santa leapt up in his sleigh. "But I never *forgot* you, Kristtörn! I searched for you at the South Pole. Every Christmas Eve. But after years of no trace, I thought it was hopeless. And as for Christmas itself—well, no one seemed to care about me anymore. First the adults stopped caring, then the children stopped writing—the joy was gone. I was alone without you." He paused somberly. "All the presents in the world couldn't fix the emptiness I felt."

"Don't blame me, you selfish man!" Kristtörn scoffed. "The children still needed you. They cared!"

The intensity of the wind grew stronger as her anger increased, and ice crystals stung their eyes as the sleigh began to shake.

"I . . . I put too much trust in others," Santa admitted. "I started doubting myself. Alpheus, my head elf, came to me one day offering to help. I was wrong to trust him, and before I knew it, Christmas had been taken away from me. At first, it was almost a relief. But when his Kringle Corporation grew in power, I knew the grave mistake I had made. Oh I'm . . . I'm so terribly sorry," he said, with tears in his eyes. "Kristtörn, can you forgive—"

But as he reached toward her with outstretched arms, he lost his balance and let go of the reins. The reindeer startled and galloped in different directions, getting lost in the swirling funnel.

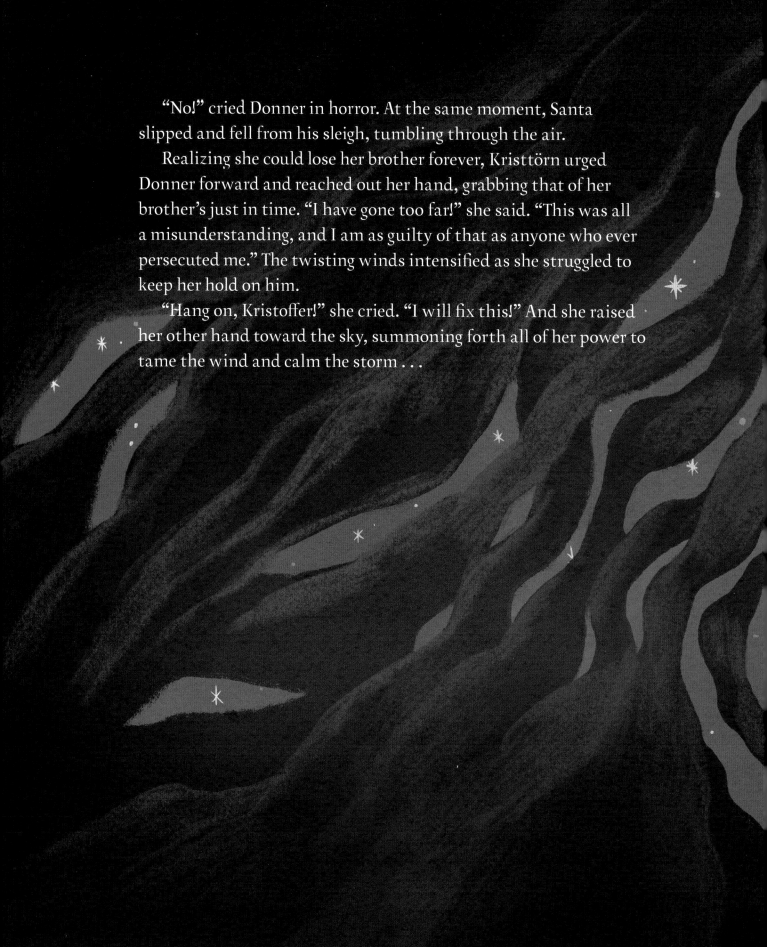

"No!" cried Donner in horror. At the same moment, Santa slipped and fell from his sleigh, tumbling through the air.

Realizing she could lose her brother forever, Kristtörn urged Donner forward and reached out her hand, grabbing that of her brother's just in time. "I have gone too far!" she said. "This was all a misunderstanding, and I am as guilty of that as anyone who ever persecuted me." The twisting winds intensified as she struggled to keep her hold on him.

"Hang on, Kristoffer!" she cried. "I will fix this!" And she raised her other hand toward the sky, summoning forth all of her power to tame the wind and calm the storm . . .

**When Poppy got home,** the house was in darkness. Her mother was still watching the news on the TV, eyes red from crying. When she saw Poppy, she reached out to hug her and gave her a kiss. "He'll be home soon. I know he will, sweetheart."

"I know he will too, Mom."

"Now you go on up to bed. Merry Christmas, Poppy."

In her room, Poppy stared out the window again, just as she had the first night that she had seen the Christmas Witch. The dense clouds parted, and for a moment she thought she saw something that looked like a shooting star, racing toward the full moon. Then it was gone . . .

"Poppy! Poppy!" The young girl opened her eyes. Her room was filled with bright light. Standing over her bed was her father!

"Dad!" she said, leaping up to give him a big hug. And she remembered—it was Christmas morning.

"Merry Christmas, Poppy! You'll never believe it—it snowed last night! And that's not all."

Just then, from outside her window, Peter called up to them.

"Dad! Poppy! Come outside! Hurry!" Poppy hopped out of bed, and she and her father ran downstairs.

The terrible fog had lifted and, in its place, a beautiful blanket of snow had covered the town, gleaming white in the morning sun. Not only that, but evergreen trees had sprung up overnight. Douglas firs, Scotch pines, blue spruces, and yes—even holly trees.

And beneath the trees, oh, *beneath the trees!* Colorful clusters
of wildflowers had miraculously sprouted and pushed their way
through the snow. Blue cornflowers, yellow buttercups, white lilies of
the valley, orange zinnias, purple violets, and of course, red poppies.
Hundreds of poppies!

All over town, families were gathered around their trees, standing
in awe of the beauty of nature. They smiled and laughed and hugged,
and sang Christmas carols and played in the snow. And there was a
feeling in the air, one that Poppy hadn't felt for a long time.

Joy! Joy was in the air. It was going to be a merry Christmas after all.

**As the glowing** rim of dawn was breaking behind the North Pole Mountains, a sleigh landed softly in the snow. A group of stable elves appeared to unharness the reindeer, leading them to graze on a patch of frozen tundra.

Donner started to follow, but then turned back. With a little bow to the Christmas Witch, he said, "My eternal thanks to you, Madam Witch!" And then he bounded off after his brothers with the excitement of a fawn.

Santa and the Witch, with the help of a few elves, carefully slid a giant block of ice off of the sleigh. Then they joined hands and placed them together upon the ice; slowly it began to melt, until Elsmere lay in a puddle on the ground. He opened his eyes to see Kristtörn holding his flipper, and he smiled. "Slippery snowcaps! What a dream I was having!" Then they embraced, tears of happiness running down her face.

"Well, what do we do now, brother?" asked the Christmas Witch.

Santa chuckled with a twinkle in his eye, one that had not been there for many a year.

"That's a question for tomorrow," he replied. "Today, we celebrate Christmas!"

**After they had** built a snowman, Poppy's parents went inside to put the Kringle Complete Frozen Holiday Meal back in the deep freezer. In honor of this special Christmas, they decided they were going to make a traditional holiday turkey with all of the trimmings—mashed potatoes, stuffing, cranberries, rolls, and a pie by Peter.

While the turkey was roasting in the oven, Poppy played her flute in the yard. As she got closer to the marshes, she saw one last little gift had been left on the rock.

*To Poppy*, the card read. *When you wear this holly crown, remember: you are never alone. We will always be connected through the earth.*
                                                                    —*The Christmas Witch*

Suddenly, a mysterious ringing came from the shed.
Poppy ran and, opening the door, found that it was coming
from the red Santa phone. She reached to answer it. A strange
voice she did not recognize greeted her on the other end . . .

**That night at** the North Pole, Kristtörn had one last dream. She was sitting with Lutzelfrau, Malachi perched on her shoulder, both staring into a roaring fire.

"So you have regained your powers, my child, just as I knew you would. And now you are reunited at last with your brother. But this is only the beginning of your journey, and there is much, much more work to be done. Christmas has been saved—for now—but there are great dangers lurking ahead . . ."

END